Jogger

Read this book?
Mark below

Special thanks to
Narinder Dhami

ORCHARD BOOKS
338 Euston Road, London NW1 3BH
Orchard Books Australia
Level 17/207 Kent Street, Sydney, NSW 2000
A Paperback Original

First published in 2008 by Orchard Books.

HiT entertainment

A CIP catalogue record for this book is available
from the British Library.

ISBN 978 1 84616 893 2
1 3 5 7 9 10 8 6 4 2

Printed in China

Orchard Books is a division of Hachette Children's Books,
an Hachette Livre UK company

www.orchardbooks.co.uk

Alice
the Tennis
Fairy

by Daisy Meadows

ORCHARD BOOKS

www.rainbowmagic.co.uk

The
Fairyland
Palace

Fairyla

Car Park

Coaches

Cooke Football
Stadium

Riding Stables

Netball Courts

Football
Pitches

Tippington
Town

LEISURE CENTRE

Swimming Pool

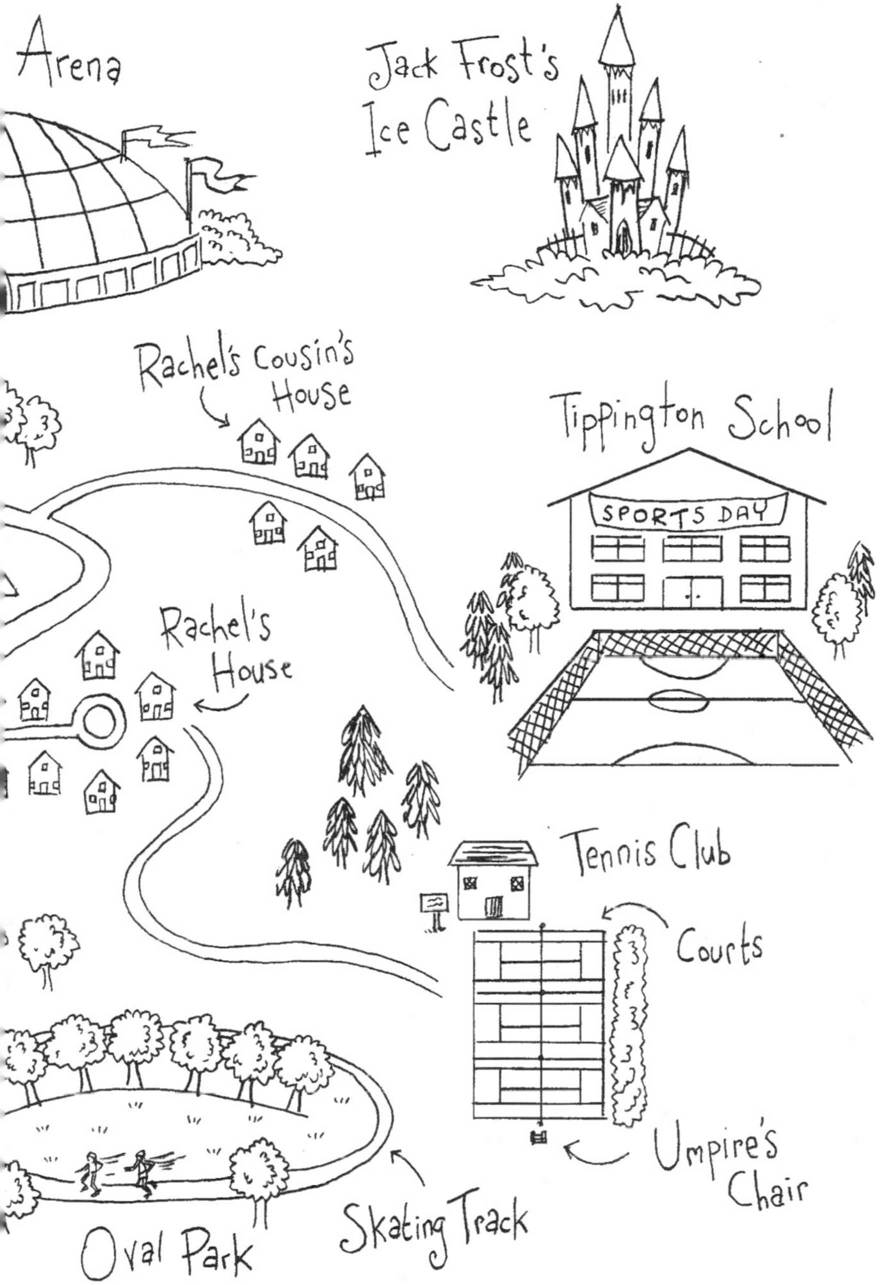

Arena

Jack Frost's Ice Castle

Rachel's Cousin's House

Tippington School

SPORTS DAY

Rachel's House

Tennis Club

Courts

Oval Park

Skating Track

Umpire's Chair

The Fairyland Olympics are about to start,
And my expert goblins are going to take part.
We will win this year, for I've got a cunning plan.
I'm sending my goblins to the arena in Fairyland.

The Magic Sporty Objects that make sports safe and fun,
Will be stolen by my goblins, to keep until we've won.
Sporty Fairies, prepare to lose and to watch us win.
Goblins, follow my commands, and let the games begin!

Contents

Goblindown

"Isn't it a gorgeous day, Kirsty?" said Rachel Walker happily. She and her best friend, Kirsty Tate, were walking along a country path not far from the Walkers' house, enjoying the sunshine. "And it would be even better if we could find another Magic Sporty Object!"

"Yes!" Kirsty agreed. "The Fairyland Olympics start tomorrow, and Alice the Tennis Fairy's Magic Racquet and Gemma the Gymnastics Fairy's Magic Hoop are still missing."

Rachel and Kirsty had promised to help their friends, the Sporty Fairies, find their seven Magic Sporty Objects. Sports in both the human and the fairy worlds were being disrupted because these objects had been stolen by Jack Frost and his goblin servants.

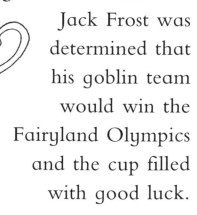

Jack Frost was determined that his goblin team would win the Fairyland Olympics and the cup filled with good luck.

He knew that the power of the Magic Sporty Objects meant that anyone close to one of them immediately became brilliant at that particular sport, so he had sent his goblins into the human world with each object, and told them to practise for the games.

As the girls walked on down the lane, Rachel suddenly noticed a strange sign pinned to a tree. "Look at that," she remarked, pointing it out to Kirsty.

Goblindon
Entrance to
Kipington
tennis club
this way →

The words on the sign had been painted very messily in bright green paint. "'*Goblindon*,'" Kirsty read aloud. "And there's an arrow with the words '*Entrance to Tippington Tennis Club – this way*' written underneath it," she added.

"Oh, no!" Rachel exclaimed. "This has got goblin mischief written all over it! Mum and I have played tennis at the club once or twice and there are always lots of people around. What if the goblins have been spotted by someone?"

Kirsty looked worried. The girls knew that nobody in the human world was supposed to find out about Fairyland and its inhabitants.

"We must find out what's going on," Kirsty said urgently. "If the goblins are at the tennis club, they might have Alice's Magic Racquet."

"Good thinking," Rachel agreed.

As the girls hurried off towards the tennis club entrance, they suddenly heard a loud voice coming from behind the hedge.

"Attention, goblins!" the voice

announced. "I shall now explain
the rules of the tournament."

"The goblins are having a tennis
tournament!" Rachel exclaimed.
"Instead of Wimbledon, it's *Goblindon!*"

"There's only one rule," the goblin
went on. "I'm the umpire in charge of
this tournament, so what I say, goes!"

He chuckled loudly, but Rachel and
Kirsty could hear the sound of other
goblins muttering and complaining.

"How many of them *are* there?"
Kirsty asked with a frown.

Rachel put a finger to
her lips. "We're right
near the tennis courts
here," she whispered.
"Let's look through
the hedge."

14

The girls pushed some leaves aside
and peered through the hedge. Both
of them tried not to gasp aloud at
the scene in front of them. Tippington
Tennis Club was full of goblins!

Tennis Time

Kirsty and Rachel glanced at each other in dismay. All the goblins were wearing tennis whites and they were limbering up as they prepared for the tournament.

"Luckily there don't seem to be any humans around," Rachel murmured.

"Look, Rachel!" Kirsty said suddenly.

"See the goblin up there on the umpire's chair?" Rachel glanced across the court and saw a big goblin standing on the umpire's chair, looking very pleased with himself. In his hand he held a pink tennis racquet that shimmered in the sunlight.

"He's got Alice's Magic Racquet!" Rachel gasped.

"We *must* try to get it back," Kirsty whispered.

"As you all know, the Goblindon tournament has been designed to perfect your tennis skills," the goblin umpire went on, "so I want to see lots of brilliant shots and some really fancy footwork! The Fairyland Olympics are coming up, and we want to beat those pesky fairies and win the cup of good luck for Jack Frost!"

All the goblins cheered as the umpire waved the Magic Racquet in the air.

"The winner of Goblindon will receive
a special prize," the umpire announced.
"He will become Keeper of the Magic
Racquet for the day!"

The goblins cheered again as they
stared longingly at the Magic Racquet.

"They *all* want to win it!" Kirsty
exclaimed.

"Yes, although I think the umpire
would rather keep
it himself,"
Rachel pointed
out, as the goblin
umpire lovingly
stroked the
racquet's pink
handle. Then he
nodded at two goblins
standing on the sidelines.

"Bring on the ball machine!" he shouted.

The goblins began to push a massive ball machine onto one end of the court, right in front of the hedge where Kirsty and Rachel were standing. The girls jumped back quickly, afraid of being seen.

"Let's go to the club entrance," Rachel whispered. "We can watch from there, and maybe we'll get a chance to grab Alice's racquet."

The girls hurried along the lane towards the tennis club gates.

As they did so, they heard the umpire explaining that, in the first round of the tournament, the goblins would be competing against the ball machine.

"Any goblin who manages to return the ball, or dodge out of the way without being hit, for a total of ten minutes, will go through to the next round," the umpire declared. "Any goblin hit by a ball will automatically be disqualified."

The girls quickly ducked behind a tree next to the club gates and peeped out.

They saw the umpire
goblin put the Magic
Racquet down carefully
on his chair and go
over to the ball
machine. The other

goblins were all gathered on
the other side of the net.

"One, two, three, go!" the umpire
yelled, switching on the machine.

It immediately began firing tennis
balls at the waiting goblins. Some of
them weren't ready and didn't even
have the chance to lift their racquets
before they were hit by flying balls.

"That's not fair!" one of them
grumbled.

"You're out!" the umpire said sternly.
The goblins who had been hit

trooped sulkily off and began filling up
the seats surrounding the court.
Meanwhile, the
remaining goblins
were batting
and lobbing
the balls away,
and just about
managing
to dodge the
ones they
couldn't return.

"Look,
Kirsty!" Rachel
nudged her friend.
"What's the umpire
doing?"

The goblin umpire was
grinning to himself.

As the girls watched, he sneakily
flipped a switch on the ball
machine and suddenly
the balls came flying
out of the machine
twice as fast.
"He's turned
the speed of
the machine
up," Kirsty
said with a
grin. "You
were right,
Rachel, he
doesn't want
any other goblin
to get the Magic
Racquet, so he's trying
to get them all out."

The goblins on the other side of the
net were now whizzing around the
court, whacking the super-fast balls
here and there.

But they hardly had time to hit
one before another was zooming
towards them.

"Hey!" one of the goblins shouted
crossly as he side-stepped a ball.

"What's going on?"

The umpire sniggered. "I said you had to practise your fancy footwork!" he shouted back. And he turned the speed up even higher.

Suddenly, one of the tennis balls spun away from the court and came heading right towards the girls.

"Kirsty, look out!" Rachel cried.

But then a very strange thing happened. The ball stopped suddenly in mid-air and hovered just in front of the tree. A tiny fairy was sitting on top of it, smiling.

"It's Alice the Tennis Fairy!" Kirsty exclaimed.

Tickets, Please!

Alice pushed back her pink visor and waved at Rachel and Kirsty. She wore matching tennis whites and pink and white trainers.

"Girls, I'm glad to see you," Alice said. "I *really* need your help to get my Magic Racquet back."

"We know where your racquet is,"

Kirsty replied. "It's on the umpire's chair."
Alice spun round and looked thrilled

as she spotted her pink,
sparkly racquet.
"How can we get
it without being
seen?" she
asked eagerly.
"Any ideas?"
"Maybe we should
sneak into the club while everyone's
distracted by the game," Rachel
suggested.

They all glanced at the court where
the remaining few goblins were still
dashing here and there.

"Good idea," Alice said.

The girls hurried through the
gates, Alice flying alongside them.

"I wonder where all the club members are," Rachel said, as they went down the path towards the clubhouse. "It's amazing that nobody has spotted the goblins yet!"

Alice grinned and pointed her wand at a poster on the clubhouse door. "That's why," she said. "There's a tournament today at Greendale Tennis Club."

"All the members must have gone to take part," Rachel agreed.

As the girls and Alice turned towards the courts, a goblin rushed out of the clubhouse. Immediately Alice hid in Kirsty's pocket.

"Stop!" the goblin shouted. He was wearing a very smart blue uniform with a peaked cap. Dismayed, Rachel and Kirsty came to a halt as the goblin stared suspiciously at them.

"Where are you going?" he snapped.

"We've come to watch the Goblindon tournament," Rachel replied bravely.

The goblin frowned, still looking suspicious. "We don't get many girls coming to watch," he said. "It's mostly just goblins. Where are your tickets?"

Rachel and Kirsty glanced anxiously

at each other. They didn't have
any tickets! But just then Kirsty felt
a tingling sensation in her pocket.
She put her hand inside and,
to her surprise, drew out
two large green tickets.
Alice was peeping out
of the pocket, too,
smiling up at her.

"Here they are,"
Kirsty said cheerfully,
handing them to the goblin.

The goblin peered at the tickets while
Rachel and Kirsty tried to hide their
grins. Both girls had realised that
Alice's fairy magic had produced
the Goblindon tickets just in time.

"These do look official," the goblin
admitted, handing the tickets back.

"OK, you can go in."

Rachel and Kirsty hurried off,
breathing sighs of relief.

"Thanks, Alice," Kirsty said as the
tiny fairy fluttered out of her pocket.
"Your magic tickets worked perfectly."

Meanwhile, Rachel had come to
a stop at one of the clubhouse windows.

"Look!" she said,
beckoning to Kirsty
and Alice. They
all peeped
through the
large window.
They could see a
huge kitchen where
two goblins, wearing aprons and chefs'
hats, were serving up strawberries and
cream into lots of different bowls.

As the friends watched, the goblins loaded the bowls onto a trolley and rolled it out of the clubhouse.

"Let's follow them and try to get the Magic Racquet back while the goblins are stuffing themselves with strawberries and cream," Kirsty whispered.

Rachel and Alice nodded, and the friends crept towards the tennis courts behind the goblins and the trolley.

Luckily the goblin audience was too caught up in what was happening on the court in front of them to notice the girls. There were only five goblins left now, battling the balls flying from the machine.

"Look, my racquet is still on the umpire's chair," Alice whispered. "I'm going to fly over and try to get it back."

"OK, but be quick, Alice," Kirsty said anxiously. "The ten minutes will be up soon."

Quickly, Alice flew off around the side of the court, keeping out of sight behind the seated goblins.

The umpire blew his whistle. "The first round of Goblindon is now over!" he announced loudly.

The goblins broke into applause and immediately the umpire headed over to his chair.

Rachel and Kirsty stared at each other in horror. Alice was heading towards the chair too, and the goblin umpire might spot her at any moment.

"We have to do something to distract him, Kirsty!" Rachel whispered. "But what?"

Double
Distraction

Thinking quickly, Kirsty pulled her
Goblindon ticket out of her skirt
pocket. "Rachel, have you got
a pen?" she asked urgently.

Rachel felt in her pockets. "Will
a pencil do?" she said, handing one
to her friend.

Kirsty nodded, took the pencil and

rushed across the court to the umpire
goblin, who was nearing his chair.

"May I have
your
autograph,
please?" she
asked,
holding out
the pencil
and her ticket.
"I think you're
the best umpire ever!"

"Oh, me too!" Rachel agreed,
realising what Kirsty was up to,
and pulling out her own ticket.
"Can I have your autograph as well?"

The goblin umpire looked very
proud of himself. "Why, of course!"
he replied with a wide smile.

As the goblin signed Kirsty's ticket, Rachel saw Alice veer away from the umpire's chair and duck behind a shrub, out of sight. Rachel sighed with relief. Kirsty's quick thinking had saved the day, but they still hadn't managed to get hold of the Magic Racquet.

Meanwhile, the umpire had finished signing autographs and was settling himself back in his chair with Alice's racquet on his lap. The girls moved to the side of the court and stood beside the trolley of strawberries and cream. As they did so, they saw one of the five winning goblins removing his white headband, replacing it with a bright orange one.

"Hey, you!" the goblin umpire shouted immediately. "You're only allowed to wear white at Goblindon. You're disqualified!"

"But that's not fair!" the goblin protested.

"Please leave the court," the umpire insisted. "You are disqualified!"

Sulkily the goblin tore off his orange headband and stomped away.

"Right, you four remaining goblins will now play a doubles match," the umpire announced. "Then the winning pair will play each other in the final, and the winner of that game will be Goblindon Champion!"

"Good work, girls," Alice whispered, zooming out of the shrub and slipping inside Kirsty's pocket as the doubles match began. "Maybe we'll get a chance to grab my racquet during this game."

The goblins were speedy and skilful, sending the ball flying across the court at different angles.

"The goblins are playing really well," Rachel murmured.

"It's only because my Magic Racquet is close by," Alice told her, as the smallest goblin dashed forward to return a low volley.

"Uh!" he grunted as he smashed the ball back across the court. Then, as it was played back to him, he hit it again with another loud grunt.

One of the goblins on the other side of  the net turned to the umpire. "He's putting me off by grunting!" the goblin declared furiously.

The umpire pointed at the smallest goblin.

"No grunting allowed at Goblindon," he said sternly. "You're disqualified!"

"That's not fair!" the smallest goblin yelled, storming off the court as the audience laughed.

His doubles partner also looked annoyed. "I'm on my own now," he complained. "Two against one isn't fair."

"Very true," the umpire agreed. He glanced at the other doubles pair. "OK, one of you has to be disqualified too, to even things up."

"Not me," declared one of the goblins, who had a very large green nose. "I'm a much better player than he is." He pointed at his partner.

"That's a fib!" his partner said
indignantly. "You're not half as good
as I am – your big nose keeps getting
in the way of your shots."

"Ooh, you take that back!" the first
goblin shouted angrily, running up to
the second goblin, who turned and ran
away across the court. The first goblin
chased after him, trying to bonk him
on the head with his racquet.

"This is the strangest tennis tournament I've ever seen!" Rachel laughed as she, Kirsty and Alice watched in amazement.

"Stop!" shouted the umpire. He pointed at the goblin with the big nose. "You're disqualified for using your racquet as a weapon," he snapped. "Leave the court!"

"No!" the goblin said sulkily.

"You can't make me!"
The umpire jumped off the chair, leaving the Magic Racquet on the seat. Rachel, Kirsty and Alice glanced hopefully at each other. "We might get a chance to grab the racquet if the umpire has to run the other goblin off the court," Kirsty whispered.

"Off! Off! Off!" chanted the crowd.

Muttering, the goblin player gave in and trudged away. To the girls' disappointment, the umpire picked up the racquet again and sat down.

"It's time for the Goblindon Final," the umpire announced, and the crowd broke into applause.

"We're not going to be able to grab the racquet while the umpire's holding it," Rachel whispered.

"We'll have to wait until the tournament's over," Kirsty sighed.

"Yes, maybe we'll get a chance when they're celebrating at the end," Alice suggested.

The girls and Alice watched as the Goblindon Final began. Both goblins were obviously determined to win, and they raced around the court, straining and stretching to return each shot.

The ball went whizzing back and forth so fast, it was a blur.

"This is going to be a very close match," Alice said anxiously. "I just hope it doesn't last too long!"

The fourth game began with a spectacular serve from one of the goblins which the other only just managed to return. The serving goblin then stumbled slightly as he hit his shot. Grinning, the second goblin leapt forward to hit the ball across the court and out of his opponent's reach, but he mistimed his shot and the ball flew into the net.

Instantly, he let out a shriek of rage. "I didn't mean to do that!" he yelled, throwing his racquet to the ground. "Someone moved the net!"

"You're disqualified for improper racquet use," the umpire declared sternly. "A racquet must only be used for hitting things."

"I *did* hit something," the goblin retorted, dancing up and down in fury. "I hit the ground!"

"That doesn't count." The umpire glared at him. "Off!"

As the goblin slunk away, his opponent punched the air gleefully. "I won!" he shouted. "I get to be Keeper of the Magic Racquet!"

The umpire looked down at Alice's racquet and frowned.

"Look, the umpire doesn't want to give the racquet away," Rachel whispered to Alice and Kirsty.

"Actually, you *haven't* won," the umpire said. "You haven't played a full match, so there *is* no winner!"

The goblin goggled at him in disbelief. "I *can't* play a full match because you've disqualified everyone else!" he pointed out furiously.

The umpire shrugged. "Well, in that case, *I'm* going to have to remain Keeper of the Magic Racquet myself," he said smugly.

As Rachel watched the goblins arguing, an idea suddenly popped into her head. She turned to Kirsty and Alice. "Whatever I say, disagree with me!" she whispered. Then she rushed over to the umpire's chair.

Kirsty and Alice glanced at each other in excitement and confusion. Rachel obviously had a plan, but what could it be?

A Winning Return

"I think this goblin is right!" Rachel said loudly. "He's the only one left in the tournament, so he should be Keeper of the Magic Racquet!"

The winning goblin looked a bit surprised, but then he grinned. "She's right!" he agreed. "I won fair and square. Hand over the racquet!"

Kirsty smiled to herself as she guessed that Rachel was trying to distract the goblins by getting them to argue with each other. "Don't let the goblins see you, Alice!" she whispered, hurrying over to the umpire.

"Well, I don't agree!" Kirsty said loudly, winking at Rachel. "It's very unfair that the other finalist got disqualified. I mean, he only threw his racquet on the ground. He's the real winner of Goblindon!"

"That's right!" the other finalist cried, darting back onto the court. "I'm a much better player than him. The racquet should be mine!"

"No, it's mine!" his opponent yelled.

"Actually, I thought it was quite unfair that the grunting goblin got disqualified too," Rachel remarked. "Everyone grunts a bit when they're playing sport."

"That's true," shouted the grunting goblin triumphantly as he rushed up to the umpire. "I'm a magnificent player! That Magic Racquet belongs to me!"

By now all the goblins in the seats were streaming onto the court, yelling and complaining. Rachel and Kirsty grinned at each other.

"I was disqualified just because I had an orange headband!" grumbled one goblin.

"Quite right, too!" retorted another.

"Silence!" screamed the umpire. "I'm in charge. My decisions are final!"

"Your decisions are rubbish!" the winning goblin jeered. "You're nothing but a muddle-headed, jelly-brained idiot!"

The umpire looked furious. He leapt down from his chair, leaving the racquet behind, and dashed over to the trolley at

the side of the court. Then he grabbed
a bowl of strawberries and cream and
tipped it over the other goblin's head.

"Help!" the
goblin shrieked
as cream ran
down his face
and the umpire
roared with
laughter.

"Alice, Rachel's
plan has worked!" Kirsty whispered as
the goblins continued to argue amongst
themselves. "Nobody's watching the
Magic Racquet. Can you grab it now?"

Alice nodded and soared up towards
the umpire's chair. None of the goblins
noticed the tiny fairy as she fluttered
down and touched the Magic Racquet.

Rachel and Kirsty watched as the racquet immediately shrank to its Fairyland size, pulsing a deeper pink colour as it did so. Alice snatched the racquet up and did a perfect backhand swing, smiling down at the girls in delight.

Kirsty grinned back. But then one of the goblins gave an angry shout.

"Look, a pesky fairy has got the Magic Racquet!" he yelled. "And I bet those naughty girls helped her to get it, too!"

Game, Set and Match

All the goblins spun round to glare at Rachel and Kirsty.

Feeling very nervous, the girls backed away as the goblins advanced.

"Oh, help!" Rachel murmured anxiously as she came to a halt against the fence at one end of the court, next to the ball machine. "Kirsty, I think we might be trapped!"

Kirsty gulped as she stared at the crowd of angry goblins heading towards them. Frantically, she glanced across the court, looking for inspiration, and her gaze fell on the food trolley.

"Alice!" Kirsty called to the tiny fairy who was hovering above the umpire's chair, looking worried. "Can you whizz the trolley over to us?"

Puzzled, Alice nodded and waved her
wand. Immediately the trolley sped over
to Rachel and Kirsty.

Straightaway, Kirsty began grabbing
bowls of strawberries and cream from
the trolley and tipping them into the
ball machine. Rachel saw what her
friend was doing and rushed to help.
Meanwhile the goblins were still
advancing menacingly.

"Here goes!" Kirsty cried when
all the bowls were empty, and
she turned the machine on.

A second later
a gooey, pink mass
of strawberries
and cream came
shooting out of
the machine.
The goblins
yelped with
surprise as they
were splattered
with the mixture
from head to toe.

"I order you to stop!"
yelled the umpire goblin.
But his words were cut short
as a large blob of strawberries

and cream flew straight into
his mouth. "Urgh!"
The umpire looked
furious, and then he
suddenly beamed
with delight.
"Yum!" he said
happily. "That
tastes lovely!"
And he began
slurping up the
strawberries and
cream from his
hands and arms.
Rachel and Kirsty
grinned at each other
as the other goblins also
began to realise that the
pink mixture tasted good.

Eagerly they scooped the strawberries and cream off themselves and crammed it greedily into their mouths.

Soon the machine was empty, but the goblins were full.

"Ooh, I'm really stuffed now," groaned the grunting goblin. "My tummy aches!"

"Mine too," the other goblins mumbled, holding their stomachs.

"Time you all went home," said
Alice, smiling kindly at them. "You'll
soon feel better."

The goblins nodded and staggered off,
clutching their bulging tummies.

"Well done, girls!" Alice laughed,
twirling around happily in the air.

"I really thought we were done for until
Kirsty had her brilliant idea to put
the strawberries and cream in the
ball machine!"

"What a mess it made, though,"
Kirsty laughed,
looking down at
the squashed
strawberries at
their feet.
"I'll soon fix
that," said Alice. And
she sent a swirl of fairy magic fizzing
across the court, cleaning up the mess in
an instant. "My magic has put
everything back to normal in the tennis
club as well," Alice went on, her eyes
twinkling, "so when the members come
back they'll never guess that there was

a Goblindon tournament here!"

"Thanks, Alice," Rachel said.

"Now I must shoot off to Fairyland and tell everyone the good news." Clutching her racquet, Alice waved to the girls. "Thank you for your help, girls, but don't forget, the Fairyland Olympics start soon and one of the Magic Sporty Objects is still missing."

"We'll do our best to find it," Kirsty promised as Alice blew them a kiss and vanished in a burst of pink sparkles.

"That was a close thing," Kirsty remarked, smiling at Rachel. "We really were outnumbered by goblins today, but we got Alice's racquet back in the end."

"And there's only Gemma the Gymnastics Fairy's Magic Hoop left to find now," Rachel added. "Kirsty, we must find it before the Fairyland Olympics start!"

"Definitely," Kirsty agreed. "But maybe we'd better go home for lunch now. All those strawberries have made me hungry!"

The Sporty Fairies

Rachel and Kirsty must now help

Gemma the Gymnastics Fairy

Without Gemma's Magic Hoop, gymnastics is being ruined for everyone *and* the goblins have a chance to win the Fairyland Olympics! Can Rachel and Kirsty help her to get it back?

Someone in School

"Almost there," Rachel Walker said as she and her best friend, Kirsty Tate, walked along the sunny street. "Aunty Joan lives around the corner, near my school."

"That's good," Kirsty said, glancing down at the basket they were carrying. "These Easter eggs might melt if it was any further!"

Kirsty was staying with Rachel's family for a week of the Easter holidays and the two girls were delivering Easter gifts to Rachel's cousins.

"I can't believe it's Friday already,"

Rachel said. "The Fairyland Olympic Games start today!"

Kirsty nodded. "And we still haven't found Gemma the Gymnastics Fairy's Magic Hoop," she said. "If we don't get it back from the goblins soon, then all the gymnastics events at the Olympics will be spoiled."

The girls were having a very exciting week, helping the Sporty Fairies find their missing Magic Sporty Objects. The Magic Sporty Objects ensured that sport was fun and safe for everyone in the human world, as well as in Fairyland, as long as they were with their rightful owners, the Sporty Fairies.

Naughty Jack Frost knew the Magic Sporty Objects were so powerful that they made anyone who was holding them, or even just close to them, very skilled at that particular sport. He had sent his goblins to steal the Sporty Objects so that they could use them to cheat in the Olympic Games and become the winning team. Jack Frost knew that the winners would receive a golden cup full of luck as the big prize – and he really wanted it for himself...

Read the rest of

Gemma the Gymnastics Fairy

to find out what magic happens next...

Have you ever wanted to name
your own Rainbow Magic Fairy?

Now is your chance to help us choose
the most magical, sparkly name
for a Rainbow Magic Fairy!*

Log on to www.rainbowmagic.co.uk
to unlock the magic within!

www.rainbowmagic.co.uk is the place to
go for games, downloads, competitions,
activities, latest news, and lots of fun!

Plus meet the fairies and find out
about their amazing adventures
with Rachel and Kirsty.

* Competition runs from April 2008 for four weeks –
please see www.rainbowmagic.co.uk for more details
For terms and conditions please see www.hachettechildrens.co.uk/terms

Win Rainbow Magic goodies!

In every book in the Rainbow Magic Sporty Fairies series (books 57-63) there is a hidden picture of a hoop with a secret letter in it. Find all seven letters and re-arrange them to make a special Sporty Fairies word, then send it to us. Each month we will put the entries into a draw and select one winner to receive a Rainbow Magic Sparkly T-shirt and Goody Bag!

Send your entry on a postcard to Rainbow Magic Sporty Fairies Competition, Orchard Books, 338 Euston Road, London NW1 3BH. Australian readers should write to Hachette Children's Books, Level 17/207 Kent Street, Sydney, NSW 2000. New Zealand readers should write to Rainbow Magic Competition, 4 Whetu Place, Mairangi Bay, Auckland, NZ. Don't forget to include your name and address. Only one entry per child. Final draw: 30th April 2009.

Good Luck!

Look out for the Music Fairies!

POPPY
THE PIANO FAIRY
978-1-40830-033-6

ELLIE
THE GUITAR FAIRY
978-1-40830-030-5

FIONA
THE FLUTE FAIRY
978-1-40830-029-9

DANNI
THE DRUM FAIRY
978-1-40830-028-2

MAYA
THE HARP FAIRY
978-1-40830-031-2

VICTORIA
THE VIOLIN FAIRY
978-1-40830-027-5

SADIE
THE SAXOPHONE FAIRY
978-1-40830-032-9

Available September 2008